DUKE'S CHASE
Do the Right Thing
Written by Laurie Zundel & Illustrated by Alice Kim

To my grandchildren,

Your lives inspire me to write and these books are written for you.

Keean, Kylie, Josh, Elijah, Jessica, Naia, Izzy, Mackenzie, Grady, Mikaela, Jaiden, Annalise, Jaxon, Corban, Abigail, and those I have yet to hold.

Live fully, love yourself and others, and enjoy the beauty in life.

I love and believe in you,
Grandma (Goga)

WEBSITE www.mytravelfriends.com
AUTHOR WEBSITE: www.lauriezundel.com
TRADEMARK My Travel Friends #8632384
COPPA APPROVED

ISBN Paperback 978-1-939347-00-8

One sunny day, Duke raced over his favorite bridge in Central Park. "I'm running late!"

"My new fetching sticks sure are heavier than my old ones. I do believe these are the most beautiful sticks in my entire collection. They should be a real hit!" Duke howled.

Duke found the perfect place for his show and hit his dog bowl with a stick to get everyone's attention.

"Hello there! I'm Duke. I'm Duke the hound.

Welcome to Central Park, the most beautiful place in all of New York City."

"Gather around this handsome, howling hound and watch me juggle the finest fetching sticks in the world! If you like my show, just throw some food scraps in my bowl," Duke howled.

"I'm Duke. I'm Duke the hound. I was rescued from the pound. You'll find me howling, yowling, prowling, growling all over town."

Everything was going perfectly and his dish was almost full, when a white cat strutted in front of him with a loud hiss.

Duke barked, "I can't believe her hissing with her nose in the air. Ruff! Will you please stop strutting? Your attitude is so irritating, I can't even concentrate!"

Duke was so distracted, he lost his balance and the sticks fell, hitting him on the head as they bounced.

BOING! CLUNCK! THUD!

"Ouch! That was a hit, in more ways than one." Then, he laughed and acted as if it were all part of his show.

The park ranger laughed so hard she dropped her nightstick.

Duke's eyes grew bigger and bigger staring as he admired, "That is the most beautiful stick I've ever seen. I don't have one like that. Oh, I want it real bad!"

In a New York second, the hound snatched it between his teeth and ran off.

"Stop! Make the right choice and give it back. Do the right thing!" The park ranger yelled as she chased him.

Duke did not listen. That was a wrong choice. So, the chase was on!

"Hide in a garden in a flowery coat."

The park ranger looked everywhere and couldn't find him anywhere! Walking around the fountain, she heard a chuckle and looked up to see Duke pretending to be an angel. She yelled, "You're no angel. Get down from there!"

He jumped down and ran across the outfield right into a baseball game. The pitcher threw the ball right when Duke was running in front of the batter.

Using the nightstick as a bat, he swung and hit a home run, ran to first base, and just kept running.

"Across the street is where I'll be,
in the Museum of Natural History."

The park ranger yelled as she chased him, "Do the right thing!"

Duke did not obey. He did not do the right thing.
Instead, he hid in an exhibit and tried to blend in.

"I'll curl my ears like a water buffalo."

WATER BUFFALO

"Use this stick as a horn like a rhino."

RHINO

"I'll be a gorilla and pound on my chest."

GORILLA

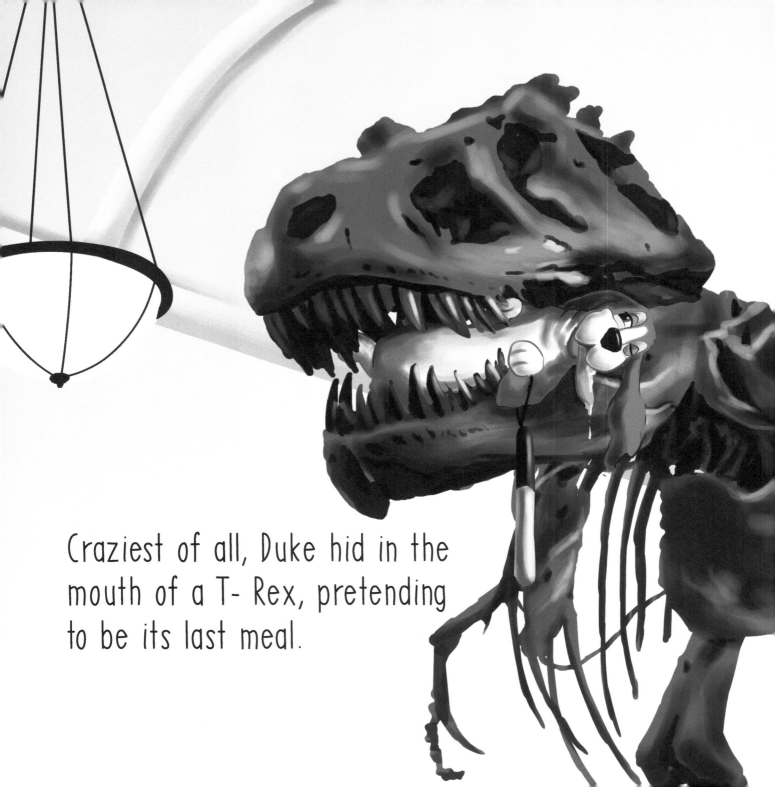

Craziest of all, Duke hid in the mouth of a T-Rex, pretending to be its last meal.

Moments later, Duke spotted a hang glider, jumped on, and flew down the busy streets of New York City.

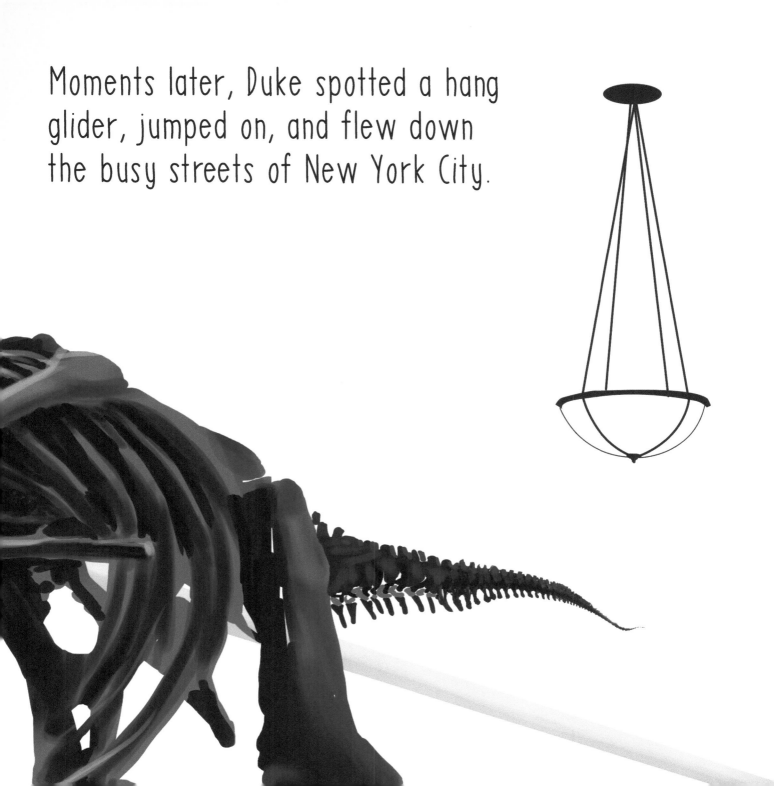

Duke soared through Times Square,

flipping and spinning through the air!

"You can fly to New York in a plane.
Take a taxi, subway, bus, or train.
The Empire State Building's down there
with Broadway, Wall Street, and Times Square."

They soared over New York Harbor and landed on top of the Statue of Liberty.

"Look at all that I can see!" Duke howled.

The Statue of Liberty came alive and whispered,
"I've seen a lot. I've watched you race. Don't you
think it's time to stop this chase?"

"Whoa!!! This is unreal!
You're a talking statue?"
Duke asked.

"A talking statue is no more unreal than a talking dog," Liberty winked. "For over 140 years, I've stood here for freedom. Duke, make good choices.

Change the world with me...
Do the right thing and you will be free!"

"I will start now. I will turn around. A new Duke's Chase is hitting the ground," he howled as he flipped down the stairs.

"I'm sorry. Will you forgive me," Duke asked.

"Yes, I forgive you," she said.

"If you forgave me, why am I here again?" Duke asked.

"There are consequences for your actions. You can choose to make this your last trip to the animal shelter," encouraged the ranger.

One moonlit night, Duke began to sing,

"How do I stop doing wrong and start doing the right thing?"

"Aha! I have a bright idea. I know the key to freedom!" Duke howled for joy.

"Make good choices and do the right thing!

I will do what is right and make a fresh start. I will do what is good and change my heart!"

"Come with me and join my team and we can all Do the Right Thing!"

Do the Right Thing Song

"I can do the right, do the right, do the right thing,
I can choose to do what's right.
I can do the right, do the right, do the right thing,
I'll make the world shine bright.
Stop and think, is it good or bad, does it help or hurt, make me happy or sad.
I can do the right, do the right, do the right thing,
I can choose to do what's right."

DISCUSSION QUESTIONS:

1. What are some of the funny things Duke does in this story?

2. Who tells Duke, "Do the right thing and be free," and what could that mean?

3. What are some ways you can make good choices?

DEAR PARENTS

I am so excited to inspire your child's imagination through My Travel Friends. My hope is to partner with you in building your child's character and expanding their knowledge and appreciation of our world.

Thank you for investing in your child, our future.

Laurie

Laurie Zundel is an innovative educator and author. Her lifelong passion is to make learning fun and encourage children to discover their unique gifts and strengths, nurturing growth and self-esteem. Nothing brings her greater joy than seeing the face of a child light up with new learning and discovery.

My Travel Friends merges her passion and love for life, children, travel, music, writing, and artistic education. Laurie uses different learning styles to build character and spread positive values. Her imaginative visuals make learning fun, and her original music makes it stick!

Laurie and her husband Larry live in Seattle and enjoy life with their growing family of 5 daughters and 15 grandchildren.

www.lauriezundel.com